Gus

Saddle Up Series
Book 32

Dave and Pat Sargent are longtime residents of Prairie Grove, Arkansas. Dave, a fourth-generation dairy farmer, began writing in early December 1990. Pat, a former teacher, began writing in the fourth grade. They enjoy the outdoors and have a real love for animals.

Gus

Saddle Up Series
Book 32

By Dave and Pat Sargent

Beyond "The End"
By Sue Rogers

Illustrated by Jane Lenoir

Ozark Publishing, Inc.
P.O. Box 228
Prairie Grove, AR 72753

Cataloging-in-Publication Data

Sargent, Dave, 1941—
 Gus / by Dave and Pat Sargent ; illustrated
by Jane Lenoir.—Prairie Grove, AR : Ozark
Publishing, c2004.
  p. cm. (Saddle up series ; 32)

 "Be thankful"—Cover.
 "SUMMARY: In Jackrabbit Junction,
Nevada a slate grullo horse helps his boss
make rounds throughout the countryside,
collecting livestock as payment for his medical
services along the way. Includes factual
information about slate grullo horses.
  ISBN 1-56763-693-4 (hc)
       1-56763-694-2 (pbk)

 1. Horses—Juvenile fiction. [1. Horses—
Fiction. 2. Physicians—Fiction. 3. Medical
care—Fiction. 4. Nevada—History—Fiction.]
I. Sargent, Pat, 1936– II. Lenoir, Jane, 1950– ill.
III. Title. IV. Series.

  PZ7.S2465Gu 2004
  [Fic]—dc21   2001007602

Inspired by

pretty slate-colored horses we see.

Dedicated to

all kids who have been lucky enough to see a beautiful slate grullo.

Foreword

Gus the slate grullo pulls a country doctor's buggy. Doc Rogers has a thriving practice in the town of Jackrabbit Junction. The farmers pay him with a rooster, a pig, a baby calf, or whatever. When a young doctor moves in, Gus gets upset. "This small town cannot support two doctors. No way! I don't always get a full ration of oats, now!"

Contents

If you would like to have the authors of the Saddle Up Series visit your school, free of charge, call 1-800-321-5671 or 1-800-960-3876.

One

Jackrabbit Junction

The shrill whistle from a train echoed across the Nevada country-side. Excited folks gathered at the depot as the train slowly chugged toward the little town of Jackrabbit Junction. Several minutes later, the steam engine rolled to a squealing halt, and the conductor stepped onto the ground.

Gus the slate grullo smiled as he trotted toward the loading dock. "I love meeting the train," he thought. "It's always exciting to see

the big steam engine and watch the
happy people."

"And Boss is always happy to get his medical supplies," he said with a chuckle.

As Gus pulled the buggy toward the loading dock, folks smiled and waved at his boss.

"Good morning, Doc."

"Howdy, Doc."

"I've been wanting to talk to you about my lumbago, Doc."

"Hi, Charlie," Doc Rogers said. "Just catch me when I'm at my office. We'll check out that lumbago for you."

Gus nodded in agreement.

"Good, Boss," he murmured. "Old Charlie is afraid you'll want to be paid if he goes to your office. His lumbago just may heal itself now!"

The slate grullo stopped beside the loading dock. He watched four or five people get off the train as his boss went into the depot. One of them was a young lady who kept glancing around as though looking for someone. Her eyes looked really frightened. "Whoa," Gus thought. "You look like you're about to have a runaway."

"Just take it easy, lady," he nickered. "We won't hurt you."

Seconds later, she fainted and collapsed on the ground.

"Boss!" Gus neighed. "That lady needs your help."

"What's happening, Gus?" a deep voice nickered.

The slate grullo looked around and saw a bay sabino trotting toward him. He was pulling a big wagon toward the train depot. Moments later, he came to a halt beside Gus.

"A lady just fell over," he said. "She seemed fine when she stepped off the train."

5

Both horses watched as a young man in a suit ran to her and knelt down. Doc Rogers joined him a moment later.

"Let me see if I can help her," he said to the young man. "I'm a doctor."

"Yes, he is," Gus murmured. "Get back and let him go to work."

"So am I," the young man said in a harsh tone. "I'll take care of her. I intend to start a practice here in Jackrabbit Junction anyway, and she can be my first patient."

"Ouch," Gus grimaced. "This is not good. Jackrabbit Junction is not big enough for two doctors. Boss and I are lucky to have beans on the table and oats in the manger."

The bay sabino shook his head and nickered, "That young doc is a real smart aleck. He's not showing your boss any respect."

"I'd be happy to kick some sense into his head," Gus snorted.

"Your boss may not appreciate your help," the bay sabino said with a chuckle. "Look. He's walking this way with a big box under one arm."

"Hey, Boss," Gus nickered. "Why aren't you taking care of that poor lady?"

Seconds later, Doc Rogers stepped up into the buggy and set the box on the seat beside him.

"Let's head back to the office, Gus," he said. "We have work to do."

"B-b-but Boss," the slate grullo muttered, "what are you going to do about that lady?"

"That young man said he's a doctor," Doc said quietly. "Surely he's able to handle a fainting spell."

Gus pawed the ground with one front hoof and snorted, "I don't like that young doctor, Boss. I don't like him at all. He's not a nice man."

"Gus Slate Grullo!" the doctor exclaimed. "You and I are going to the office so I can put all my medical supplies in order. Let's go!"

"Yessir, Boss," Gus grumbled as he turned away from the train depot. "I'll go. But I don't have to like it."

Two

Apple Pie for Gus? Yuck!

The sun was overhead, as Gus dozed at the hitching post in front of the office. Suddenly a sorrel skidded to a stop beside the buggy. A boy leaped off the sorrel's back and ran up the stairs toward Doc Rogers' office.

"Doc! Doc Rogers!" the boy yelled. "Come quick!"

Gus looked at the sorrel and asked, "Are you okay?"

"Yes," the sorrel nickered with a nod of his head. "But the father of my young boss is hurt."

Doc Rogers ran down the stairs with the young boy following.

"How bad is he hurt?" Doc asked the boy as he climbed into the buggy.

"I don't know," the youngster replied as he jumped onto the back of the sorrel. "Ma just told me that Pa is hurt and that I had to come and get you."

"This sounds like it could be serious," Gus murmured as he loped down Main Street with the buggy bouncing along behind him.

Twenty minutes later, Gus and the sorrel stopped beside the barn door at the Olsen farm. The slate grullo watched his boss run inside with his little black bag clutched in one hand. He peeked through the door and saw Mr. Olsen lying on a

pile of hay. One leg was bent at a
strange angle.

"Well now, Mr. Olsen," Doc said as he kneeled down beside him. "It looks like you've broken your leg. How did it happen?"

"I was in the hayloft, Doc," the man groaned. "I stepped backward, and well, the next thing I knew I was lying here on the floor."

Doc looked up toward the hayloft with a faint smile and muttered, "It would have been better if you had used the ladder, Mr. Olsen. It would not have been so painful."

"Thanks a bunch, Doc," the man growled. "But since I didn't, can you fix my leg?"

"Sure," Doc said soothingly. "You'll be fine in eight weeks."

"Eight weeks!" the man yelled. "Doc, I have too much work to do. I can't be off my leg for two months.

Who'll feed the livestock and plow the fields?"

"That boy of yours can do it," Doc said as he put a splint on the broken leg. "You'll be fine. Now let's get you into the house where you'll be more comfortable."

Almost two hours later, Doc was getting into the buggy when Gus saw the lady of the house run toward them with a pie in her hands.

"Wait a minute, Doc," she called out. "I want to pay you for helping my husband."

She handed the pie to him and said, "Thanks a lot, Doc. I'm sorry we don't have any money to give you. But I hope you like apple pie."

"Humph," the grullo muttered. "Why didn't you just give him the apples? I like those a bunch."

"This pie is perfect pay for my services, Mrs. Olsen," Doc said with a smile. "Thank you."

While they were on their way back to Jackrabbit Junction, Doc suddenly said, "We better go by Smith's farm and see how Mr. Smith is doing with that sprained ankle."

"Sure, Boss," Gus agreed. "We really should do that."

An hour later, the slate grullo trotted away from the Smith farm. Mr. Smith was grateful to the doctor for stopping by and gave him a rooster as pay for his assistance. The rooster now stood in a cage beside the pie which was next to the doctor on the front seat of the buggy. And every few minutes, the happy rooster sang to Gus and his boss.

"Cock-a-doodle-doo!"

"I just remembered something, Gus," Doc yelled above the crowing. "We need to stop by the Jones farm. Her baby is due any day now."

"Yessir, Boss," the slate grullo replied. "I'm on my way there."

As Gus and the buggy with the crowing rooster stopped in front of the house, a man ran out.

"Doc!" he yelled. "I was just coming to get you. My wife is about to have her baby."

Three hours later, Doc got back into the buggy and said, "Okay, Gus. Let's go home."

"Wait, Doc!" Mr. Jones yelled from the doorway. "I haven't paid you for delivering my baby son."

Around fifteen minutes later, Gus was pulling the buggy down the road toward town. The pie sat on the seat beside Doc, the rooster stood in his cage next to the pie, and a calf trotted behind the buggy.

"Moo! Moo!" the calf called.

"Cock-a-doodle-doo!" the rooster sang.

"Oh my," Gus groaned. "I hope Boss is through with his house calls. It's getting a bit noisy around here."

Three

The Menagerie

The slate grullo breathed a sigh of relief as he walked down the road toward Jackrabbit Junction.

"Thank goodness, we're almost home," he mumbled amid the sound of the bawling calf and the crowing rooster. "And I am sure glad."

Suddenly a young girl ran toward them. "Doc!" she yelled. "Mama said to come quick. My brother just fell out of a tree."

"Lead the way," Doc Rogers said. "We'll follow you."

One hour and ten minutes later, Gus pulled the buggy back onto the road toward Jackrabbit Junction. The grateful parents of the boy with the broken arm had paid Doc well. A big woolly sheep was now tied beside the calf behind the buggy.

"Baaa! Baaa! Baaa!"

"Moo! Moo! Moo!"

"Cock-a-doodle-doo!"

"Let's try this again, Gus!" the doctor shouted. "Are you ready to go home?"

Before Gus had a chance to nod his head, a man stopped in front of him.

"Doc Rogers," he yelled above the sound of the rooster, the calf, and the sheep. "Would you take a few minutes to check my little girl? She has a high fever."

"A fever can be really serious," Doc shouted. "Let's go take a look at her."

Forty-five minutes later, Doc walked from the house toward Gus.

"That little gal has the chicken-pox, Gus," he said with a chuckle. "You know what that means."

The slate grullo nodded his head and groaned.

"Oh dear," he nickered softly. "It means every child in the territory is going to need my boss for the next few weeks."

Suddenly the father of the little girl approached the buggy. He was leading a pig on a rope.

"Doc," he yelled above the sound of the animals tied to the buggy. "I have six more kids who'll be coming down with the chicken-pox. I want you to have this pig as payment for taking care of them."

"I thank you, Mr. Adams," Doc shouted. "Gus and I will be glad to check on your kids every few days."

After the pig was secured to the buggy between the calf and the sheep, Gus, once again, headed for town.

The sun was setting on the western horizon as Gus approached the office of Doc Rogers.

"Moo! Moo! Cock-a-doodle-doo! Baa! Baa! Oink! Oink!"

Suddenly the slate grullo saw the young doctor who had come to town on the train that morning. His eyes and mouth were wide open with shock as he hurried toward them.

"What's all of that?" he shouted as he pointed to the pie and all the animals.

Doc smiled and yelled, "That, Sir, is my pay for the day."

"Doesn't anybody use money to pay for your medical services here?" the young doctor asked in a loud voice.

"No, sonny," Doc Rogers said. "Nobody can afford to pay cash for medical treatments around here. But they are good honest hard-working folks, and they pay what they can." He waved his hand toward the pie, the rooster, the calf, the sheep, and the pig. "This is my pay for a day's work."

"That does it," the young doctor said. "I'm going back east."

"Hmmm," Gus thought. "Boss is one smart man. I know now that

he wasn't really worried about hav-
ing a new doctor come to town."

"I believe that country doctors will be important to folks throughout history. Hmmm, but I wonder if folks will remember a slate grullo named Gus who was this doctor's best friend and partner? It doesn't really matter. Life for this country-doctor's horse is just great!"

Four

Slate Grullo Facts

Grullo, which is pronounced GREW-yo, is the Spanish name for the sandhill crane, which is a slate-colored bird. The name *grullo* is used by western riders when they refer to a blue slate-colored horse with black points and a dark head. *Blue dun* and *mouse dun* are English terms. They are used in England when describing a horse of the same color. A slate grullo is a usual grullo color. The body is tan or slate, and the head is dark.

Slate Grullo

There are times when the body color of a grullo can occur because of environmental changes. Slate grullos fade to olive grullo in strong sunlight. Some olive grullos are always olive and are not faded slate grullos.

Olive Grullo

Ancestral colors in the wild horse of Poland, called Tarpan, are responsible for the different shades of grullos that we have today.

The Tarpan

BEYOND "THE END"

How do you catch a loose horse?
Make a noise like a carrot.
British Cavalry Joke

WORD LIST
apple pie
slate grullo
corn
bay sabino
pig
star
rooster
sorrel
stripe
oats
Conestoga
calf
chestnut
grass

37

sheep
black
salt
blaze

From the word list above, write:

1. One word that names a breed of horse.

2. Three words that tell markings on a horse.

3. Four words that tell foods a horse eats.

4. Five words that tell the color of horses.

5. Five words that name payments given to Dr. Rogers for his doctoring services. Was this fair payment for the country doctor?

CURRICULUM CONNECTIONS

This story took place in 1820: True or False ? Give a reason for your answer.

If you are not sure, check out the wonderful website on railroad steam engines, dates of inventions, weights—from less than one ton to 600 tons, interesting history, pictures, and sounds of trains at <www.members.aol.com/vlcondon/index. htm>.

There are two museums in the U.S. honoring the work of men like Dr. Rogers: one is in North Carolina and one is in Arkansas. Visit the Arkansas Country Doctor Museum at website <www. drmuseum.net>.

What kind of buggy did the country doctor in Arkansas have? Do you suppose Gus pulled the same kind for Dr. Rogers?

A seven-year-old horse is considered mature.

How old is this in a man's age if a year of a horse's life is equivalent to three years of a man's?

PROJECT

Combine your math and artistic skills! Draw to scale and accurately color a picture (body, tail, and mane) of the horse that is featured in each book read in the Saddle Up Series. You could soon have sixty horses prancing around the walls of your classroom!

Learning + horses = FUN.

Look in your school library media center for books about how to draw a horse and the colors of horses. Don't forget the useful information in the last chapter of this book (Slate Grullo Facts) and the picture on the book cover for a shape and color guide.

HELPFUL HINTS AND WEBSITES
A horse is measured in hands. One hand equals four inches. Use a scale of 1" equals 1 hand.

Visit website <www.equisearch.com> to find a glossary of equine terms, information about tack and equipment, breeds, art and graphics, and more about horses. Learn more at <www.horse-country. com> and at <www.ansi.okstate.edu/breeds/horses/>.

KidsClick! is a web search for kids by librarians. There are many interesting websites here. HORSES and HORSE-MANSHIP are two of the more than 600 subjects. Visit <www.kidsclick.org>.

Is your classroom beginning to look like the Rocking S Horse Ranch? Happy Trails to You!

ANSWERS (1. False—The first railroad steam engine was built in 1829. 2. A Studebaker buggy. 3. 21 years old.)